Praise for *I'd Rather Be Me*

"*I'd Rather Be Me* is a wonderful celebration of individuality and self-expression. With beautiful illustrations and a heartwarming message, this book gently guides children to embrace their uniqueness with courage and confidence. An essential addition for any young reader's bookshelf, inspiring them to shine bright in the world!"

—Nima Patel, founder of Mindful Champs, parenting coach, and author of the picture book *The Best You*

"*I'd Rather Be Me* is a much-needed, child-friendly antidote to the photo-filtered and social-media-worthy world we live in that glamorizes changing oneself to fit in or be cool. Our messaging to children should be to celebrate, cherish, and have confidence in their uniqueness, and this book does just that!"

— Christina Furnival, licensed professional clinical counselor, mom of three, and author of the award-winning Capable Kiddos series

I'D RATHER BE ME

Story by
Emily Peace Harrison

Art by
Dacil Curbelos

BELLE ISLE BOOKS
www.belleislebooks.com

Copyright © 2024 by Emily Peace Harrison

No part of this book may be reproduced in any form or by any electronic or mechanical means, or the facilitation thereof, including information storage and retrieval systems, without permission in writing from the publisher, except in the case of brief quotations published in articles and reviews. Any educational institution wishing to photocopy part or all of the work for classroom use, or individual researchers who would like to obtain permission to reprint the work for educational purposes, should contact the publisher.

ISBN: 978-1-962416-24-5

Library of Congress Control Number: 2024900406

Designed by Sami Langston
Production managed by Ceci Hughes

Printed in the United States of America

Published by
Belle Isle Books (an imprint of Brandylane Publishers, Inc.)
5 S. 1st Street
Richmond, Virginia 23219

BELLE ISLE BOOKS
www.belleislebooks.com

belleislebooks.com | brandylanepublishers.com

To Casey and Cole—you have always been my endless source of inspiration. I hope that you look at me and feel inspired too—inspired to never give up on your goals. Every day is a new opportunity to make your dreams come true. I love you both more than you could ever know.

—Mom

Hank was a pup, happy and free,

with one little problem—a tiny flea.

He buzzed in Hank's ear as loud as could be,

Asking the question, "Who would you be?"

"If you were not you,

who would you be?"

"Maybe a whale in the deep blue sea?"

"I'd rather be me,"

Hank said to the flea.

"Or a beautiful bird, flying high as can be,

would be very exciting! Don't you agree?"

"I'd rather be me,"

Hank said to the flea.

"A monkey in the jungle, who swings on the trees?

Now that would be fun, I can guarantee!"

"I'd rather be me,"

Hank said to the flea.

"Then maybe a lion, who runs wild and free,

or a hippo, or turtle, or bumble bee?"

"I'd rather be me,"

Hank said to the flea.

"If you were living in a zoo, you could hang out with kangaroos!

I hear they're very bourgeoisie, eating scones and drinking tea.
Now that sounds pretty good to me!"

Hank shook his head twice,
and off flew the flea.

"Now listen up, flea!

Listen to me!"

"I like who I am! I want to be me!

Not a bird, not a whale, nor a chimpanzee."

"So, you be you, and I'll be me . . .
the very best flea and me we can be!"

About the Author

Emily Peace Harrison was the youngest of five children in a house full of glorious chaos. It is no surprise that she established a career as the ultimate organizer of chaos, serving as an executive assistant in higher education for over fifteen years. Having had a front-row seat to the emotional journeys of her four siblings, her two sons, and countless college students (not to mention her own personal journey), Emily knows the importance of character building in the early stages of a child's life as a way to prepare them for the emotional struggles they are sure to face. Beginning with her debut, *I'd Rather Be Me*, Emily's picture books, filled with beautiful illustrations and heartfelt characters, aim to inspire confidence, foster empathy, and promote self-esteem in young readers. When she's not at her day job or crafting rhymes for her stories, Emily enjoys stirring up a little chaos of her own with family and friends.

Printed in the USA
CPSIA information can be obtained
at www.ICGtesting.com
CBHW061921270824
13786CB00011B/128